This book belongs to:

The CYCLOPS WITCH

and the HEEBIE-JEEBIES

Written by KYLE SULLIVAN
Illustrated by DEREK SULLIVAN

HAZY DELL PRESS

Portland • Seattle

To our nephew, Luca Edward.

Find all Hazy Dell Press books at www.hazydellpress.com

10 9 8 7 6 5 4 3 2 1 / Printed in China / 978-1-948931-00-7

ot much could frighten the Cyclops Witch.

Nor make her

shiver,

quïver,

or **twitch.**

Not the freezing ice troll
she stared down cold,

nor the leprechaun
she tricked out of gold.

Not the pumpkinhead
she dueled with a fork,

nor the winged monkeys
she fled on a stork.

Not much made her shiver, quiver or twitch,
but this witch's courage had one small hitch.

One thing gave her the creeps and made her skin crawl—
though she'd never once met it. Not once at all.

Until one night…

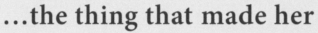

…the thing that made her

shiver,

quiver,

and **twitch…**

…walked right up to the door of the Cyclops Witch.

From her door there came a tapping—the witch spilled her tea!
"'Tis some visitor," she gasped. "Whoever could it be?"

"Let's not panic, my dear," quoth the raven, Lenore.
"There's a very good chance it's a friend at the door."

She creeped up to her peephole and tensely peeped out—
what she peeped left her deeply, intensely creeped out!

Her scariest nightmare had finally come true…

Staring back at her were kids…exactly like you.

She blitzed out her back window, running like mad.
"Gah! Children!" she shrieked. "This is so very bad!

"They're so nasty and weird and wild and mean!
"Always dripping in mud—gross and unclean!

"They'll tickle! And roughhouse! And pinch! And bite!
"Come on, Cyclops Witch! Let's put up a fight!"

Behind a rock she tumbled and trembled with fear.
"Whatever could they want?! Why oh why are they here?!"

"They seem nice to me," quoth Lenore with a wink.
"Not funny!" cried the witch. "I really must think!"

The witch puzzled and pondered a way out of her bind.
Then suddenly, like thunder, a plan rolled through her mind.

"I'll lure them through Hazy Dell toward Swirlwind Bay,
"and all the creepy beasties will scare them away!

"If the first three creatures aren't enough to do the trick,
"the awful ancient sea beast will surely scare them sick!"

She popped out from the rock with a crazy yell:
"Follow me—if you dare—into Hazy Dell!"

"Don't run!" cried the children. "Come back here, please!"
But swiftly, she vanished, into the trees.

She ran to the shadows of the hobgoblin's lair.
"This silly little stinker should give them a scare!"

Behind a mildewy tree she waited with glee—
but then a strange thing happened she didn't foresee...

The children weren't scared of the hobgoblin at all!
They were roasting marshmallows and having a ball!

As they sipped cocoa and swigged apple cider,
the Cyclops Witch gawked, and her eye grew wider.

"I can't BELIEVE they weren't scared," she said with a scoff.
"But the vampire will certainly scare them right off!"

At the vampire's castle she ducked low and waited—
but what she saw next left her sad and deflated...

The children weren't scared—they were hopping and whooping around a vampire who was happily hooping!

As they twirled and whirled, somersaulted and tumbled, the witch scowled and grunted and grumpily grumbled.

She grumbled all the way
to the mothman's hut.
"The mothman will scare'em
and show'em what's what!"

She ducked down to hide
behind a rusty car door—
then, the kids showed up,
and her jaw dropped to the floor...

They weren't running with fear, they were stargazing!
They oohed and they aahed at stars that were blazing!

As they told tales of creatures in far-off lands,
the Cyclops Witch groaned with her head in her hands.

"This is NOT happening!" she bitterly hissed.
She glared toward the sea with a tightly clenched fist.

"It's as if they're all friends! They aren't scared in the least!
"But NOBODY'S not scared of the ancient sea beast!"

She scuttled to the end of a long sea jetty,
and scrunched down by a buoy, quiet and ready.

There was a sound.

She gasped.

Her heart skipped a beat.

The witch and the kids had been swept off their feet!

Dripping tentacles gripped them over the ocean,
and the Cyclops Witch moaned with woeful emotion:

"Oh no! What a world! Is this really the end?
"Farewell, dear Lenore. You've been such a good friend."

But wait! The beast had politely lowered them down.
"Pardon me," she said. "I was just messing around."

Said a child to the witch, in a voice strong and clear:
"We're the Heebie-Jeebies, you have nothing to fear.

"We travel the world, over mountain, sea and prairie,
"to help others overcome the things they find scary.

"Your friend Lenore reached out and requested our service.
"You were so scared of kids, it was making her nervous."

"Aw, Lenore," said the witch. "Did you do this for me?"
Quoth the raven: "Of course! That's what friends do, silly."

"We'd like to help you," said the child, "sort the fake from the true.
"Just like we helped four monsters on our way to helping you!

"On our way to your door, through the Bay and the Dell,
"we helped them face their fears—and have some fun as well!

"In fact...

"Maria helped the hobgoblin
be cool around fire,

"and with Germaine's help,
exercising's fun for Vampire.

"Hector helped the mothman
be stress-free in the dark,

"and I helped the sea beast
become friends with a shark.

"And that's how Heebie-Jeebies earn our sashes and ears—

"by compassionately helping friends conquer their fears.

"While not all fears are bad, some can get out of hand—
"sometimes we're just scared because we misunderstand.

"You see, your fear of children is not based on facts.
"Once you get to know us, you'll completely relax."

The witch eyeballed the kids with her probing eyeball…
"Well," she said. "You don't seem loud or dirty at all.

"And you don't roughhouse or pinch or tickle or bite…
"Could I have had it all wrong? Could you be all right?

"I can't believe it. You're brave, kind, and clever too…

"You're exactly like me! I'm exactly like you!"

Now nothing could frighten the Cyclops Witch.
Nothing made her shiver, quiver or twitch.

Without any fears, without any scares,
she chose to help her peers overcome theirs.

She helped the ice troll
embrace the warm sunlight,

and helped the leprechaun
defeat his stage fright.

She helped the pumpkinhead
approach his teenage daughter,

and helped the winged monkeys
loosen up in the water.

She helped these creatures and many creatures more.
…Then, one day, there came a tapping at her door.

The witch giggled and gently set down her tea.
"'Tis some visitor," she laughed. "Who could it be?"

"Whoever it is," quoth the raven with a grin.
"Promise me you won't make a getaway again!"

"It's a deal!" smirked the witch, who calmly opened the door…

…to find beaming Heebie-Jeebies and monsters galore!

Said Latasha: "By helping friends defeat their fears,
"you have earned your Heebie-Jeebies sashes and ears."

Wiping a tear, the witch declared with delight:
"Your compassion helped me overcome my fright.

"I'm a much happier witch without fear in my heart…

"Nearly missing your friendship was the scariest part!"